Beautiful Boys

By: Michelle Jones-Freeman

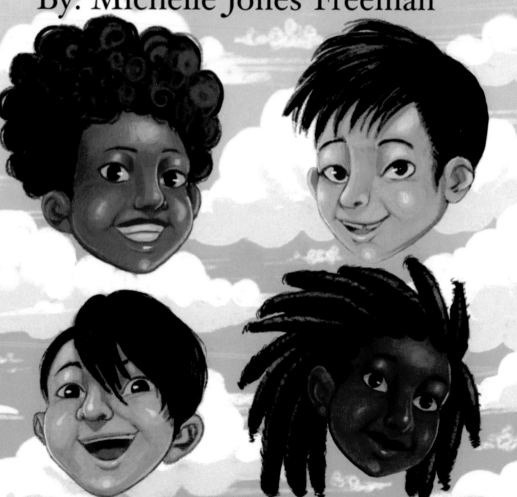

Beautiful Boys

Michelle Jones-Freeman

Published by: Free Amanda & Co.

Book Cover & Illustrations by: Shaniya Carrington

Printed in the United States of America

U.S. Copyright #1-10595293391
ISBN: 978-1737426707

A story inspired by my publisher and the desire to

express to young black boys everywhere how much they

are loved. God loves you and so do I!

As a mom of four girls, it goes without saying that moms who raise sons are faced with many different challenges, primarily black and brown sons.

I dedicate this book to my three nephews, Law, Beau & Ahmad.

I dedicate this to my Godson Jaylen.

I dedicate this to my spiritual son, Kristopher.

With that, this book is for every mom raising a boy to be a productive man.

I stand with you in prayer for you.

This is for every boy.

"if God is for you, who or what can be against you."

Romans 8:31

The song goes,
"Beautiful, beautiful boy."
What joy you bring to me.

My boy, my son,
Nubian Prince, and
Brown king.
What joy and delight
you bring.

My beautiful, beautiful boy.
I pray you dream and live big.

I hold you close
And gaze at you deep.
My beautiful boy, please don't weep.

My beautiful beautiful boy
I will teach you what I know.
I will protect you and pray that
God's wisdom will overflow.

My beautiful, beautiful boy
With dark skin and brown eyes.
The world wants to harm you,
But I'll stand by your side.

My love runs deep
It blocks every trap against you.
Fear not
For the lord is with you.

My beautiful, beautiful boy
Society wants to hide you.
I want to guide you,
But God will provide for you.

My beautiful,
Beautiful boy,
The crown
Is on your head.

Royalty in your dreads;
Abundance in your portion is fed.

My beautiful, beautiful boy
You can wear your hair cut, trimmed
or shaved.

You can have dreadlocks, a ponytail,
Or luscious braids.

Your worth and value
Have already paved the way.
Your uniqueness can't be hidden
Behind the shade.

My beautiful, beautiful boy
Don't be scared, sad, or feel lost

Take pride in who you are.
Your beautiful skin tells the story of an
Undeniable war.

My beautiful, beautiful boy
The fight is not with you
The struggle is in you
The battle is for you.
Success is all you.

My beautiful, beautiful boy,
Be who you are!

Hold your head high,
And let your mind drift far!

Let your fingers be the guard.
You are mighty, wonderful,
The brightest of stars.

So shine bright, my king, my prince,
And let love erase every scar.

Beautiful boy,

You are loved to the moon and back!

Know that, own that,
Walk in that.

And that is that.

The End!

Author's Bio

Michelle Jones - Freeman is the mother of four girls. A Brooklyn, N.Y. native, she was first introduced to writing as an undergrad student at John Jay College of Criminal Justice where she earned a B.A. in Forensic Psychology and a M.A. in Criminal Justice. Writing children stories became her passion after becoming a mom to her first born. Motherhood provides lots of creative expressions and materials to share. Still very new to the author scene, she has published, Mommy says, "I love you", and now excited to present her latest book, Mommy says. She is also the co-author of the upcoming blog titled, "Anointed Conversations". Michelle hopes that parents will enjoy these stories of love and motherhood through her lens.

If you would like to know more about Michelle and when her next books will be available, and her upcoming blog, please feel free to reach her at amandamich12@gmail.com or at info@anointedconversations.org.

Contact

If there are any questions, comments, or inquiries about
bulk purchases and speaking engagements,
please contact me at:

Free Amanda and Co.
amandamich12@gmail.com

Made in the USA
Middletown, DE
29 March 2022

63373300R00020